Make a Shiny Crown

written by Anne Giulieri

photography by Ned Meldrum

Look at the *crown* on the king's *head*.

A crown is on the queen's head too!

Sea horses have a crown.

The crown is on top of a sea horse's head.

It is not like ·a king's or queen's crown.

crown

You can make a crown.

To make a crown get:

scissors

cut-up foil

glue and brush

paper

yellow paper, red paper, and green paper

tape

shapes

pencil

circle

diamond

square

Get the paper and the scissors.
Fold the paper like this.

Cut the paper
into two *rectangles*.

Next make
a long rectangle.

Get the *foil* and the glue.

Glue the foil on the paper like this.

Then cut *triangles*
into the paper
and the foil.

Then cut the red paper
into little *circles*.
The little red circle
looks like a *ruby*
on a ring.

Next cut the green paper into little *squares*.
The little green square looks like an *emerald* on a ring.

Next cut the yellow paper
into little *diamonds*.
The little yellow diamond
looks like a diamond
on a ring.

Glue the red circles
on to your crown.
Glue the green squares
and yellow diamonds
on to your crown.

13

You can ask your teacher
to help you place
the crown on your head.

You can make
a crown with *stars*
and *feathers* too.

Picture Glossary

sea horses

circles

emerald

head

squares

crown

feathers

rectangles

stars

diamonds

foil

ruby

triangles